The Primary Source Library of the Thirteen Colonies and the Lost Colony ™

The Colony of South Carolina

A Primary Source History

PowerKids Press
PRIMARY SOURCE

Melody S. Mis

To my big sis, Linda Wightman Meyer

Published in 2007 by The Rosen Publishing Group, Inc.
29 East 21st Street, New York, NY 10010

First Edition

Editor: Jennifer Way
Book Design: Ginny Chu
Layout Design: Julio Gil
Photo Researcher: Amy Feinberg

Photo Credits: Cover, pp. 8 (right), 16 (right) © North Wind Picture Archives; p. 4 (left) Service Historique de la Marine, Vincennes, France, Lauros/Giraudon/Bridgeman Art Library; p. 4 (right) The George A. Howard Collection; p. 6 (left) © The Image Works; pp. 6 (right), 10 (left), 12 (left) South Carolina Department of Archives & History; pp. 8 (left), 14, 20 (left) The New York Public Library/Art Resource, NY; p. 10 (right) Library of Congress; pp. 12 (right), 18 (right) Private Collection, The Stapleton Collection/Bridgeman Art Library; pp. 16 (left), 18 (left) National Portrait Gallery, Smithsonian Institution/Art Resource, NY; p. 20 (right) © Chicago Historical Society, Chicago, USA/Bridgeman Art Library.

Library of Congress Cataloging-in-Publication Data

Mis, Melody S.
    The colony of South Carolina : a primary source history / Melody S. Mis.
        p. cm. — (The primary source library of the thirteen colonies and the Lost Colony)
    Includes index.
    ISBN 1-4042-3438-1 (library binding)
    1. South Carolina—History—Colonial period, ca. 1600–1775—Juvenile literature. 2. South Carolina—History—1775–1865—Juvenile literature. 3. South Carolina—History—Colonial period, ca. 1600–1775—Sources—Juvenile literature. 4. South Carolina—History—1775–1865—Sources—Juvenile literature. I. Title. II. Series.
    F272.M57 2007
    975.7'02—dc22
                                    2005030179

Manufactured in the United States of America

Contents

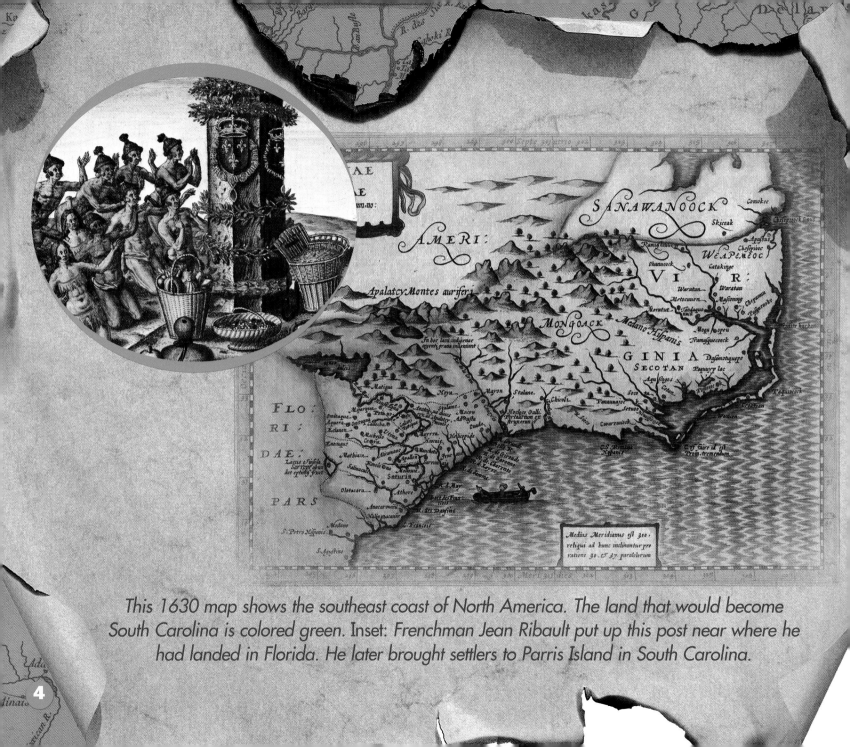

This 1630 map shows the southeast coast of North America. The land that would become South Carolina is colored green. Inset: Frenchman Jean Ribault put up this post near where he had landed in Florida. He later brought settlers to Parris Island in South Carolina.

Discovering South Carolina

Native Americans had lived in South Carolina long before Europeans came. The Native Americans living there included the Cherokee, the Yamassee, and the Catawba.

The first European to see the South Carolina coast was the Spaniard Francisco Gordillo in 1521. Five years later Lucas Vasquez de Ayllon, from the Dominican Republic, sent 500 people to South Carolina, but the colony failed. In 1562, the Frenchman Jean Ribault and 150 settlers landed on Parris Island, off the coast of South Carolina. The settlers did not know how to grow food, and they almost died of hunger. In 1563, the French settlers left the colony and returned to France. Nearly 150 years passed before a lasting colony was established in South Carolina.

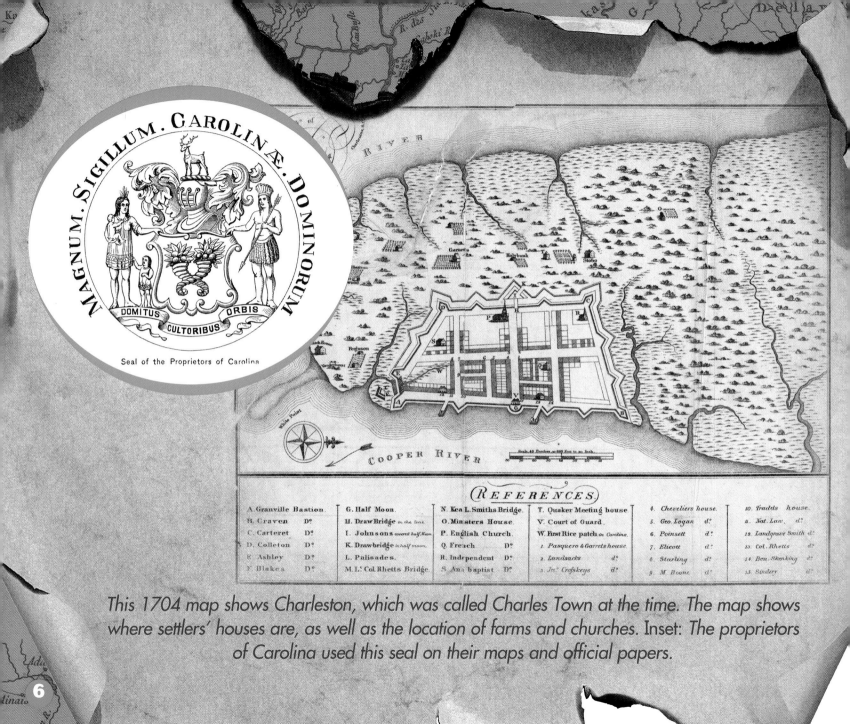

REFERENCES

A. Granville Bastion.	G. Half Moon.	N. Kea L. Smiths Bridge.	T. Quaker Meeting house.	4. Cheveliers house.	10. Tradds house.
B. Craven Dº.	H. Draw Bridge in the line.	O. Minsters House.	V. Court of Guard.	5. Geo. Logan dº.	11. Nat. Law. dº.
C. Carteret Dº.	I. Johnsons covered half Moon.	P. English Church.	W. First Rice patch in Carolina.	6. Poinsett dº.	12. Landgrave Smith dº.
D. Colleton Dº.	K. Drawbridge in half moon.	Q. French Dº.	1. Pasquero & Garrets house.	7. Elicott dº.	13. Col. Rhetts dº.
E. Ashley Dº.	L. Palisades.	R. Independent Dº.	2. Landsacks dº.	8. Starling dº.	14. Ben. Skenking dº.
F. Blakes Dº.	M. Lt Col. Rhetts Bridge.	S. Ana baptist Dº.	3. Jnº Crofskeys dº.	9. M. Boone dº.	15. Sindery dº.

Seal of the Proprietors of Carolina

This 1704 map shows Charleston, which was called Charles Town at the time. The map shows where settlers' houses are, as well as the location of farms and churches. Inset: The proprietors of Carolina used this seal on their maps and official papers.

Founding the Twelfth Colony

In 1629, Charles I, king of England, gave land in North America to Robert Heath. Heath named his land Carolina after the king. Heath did not have enough money to establish a colony there, though. In 1663, Charles II gave Carolina to eight Englishmen. They set up a **proprietary colony**. They wanted to make money by selling or renting land in South Carolina to settlers.

In 1670, the proprietors sent William Sayle and more than 100 people to South Carolina. They came from the English settlement on the island of Barbados in the Caribbean Sea. The colonists established the twelfth colony. It was called Charleston. Sayle became the colony's first governor. After Charleston had been established, more people from England and Barbados began to move there.

Many early settlers in South Carolina built homes near rivers and other bodies of water.
Inset: Malaria is an illness that is passed on by mosquitoes. This was not discovered until the
nineteenth century. Mosquitoes are common in warm, wet areas, such as South Carolina.

Settling South Carolina

The English began to settle in South Carolina in the 1670s. The first settlers in South Carolina lived in tents until they could clear the land of trees. Then they built homes. They also planted corn, sugarcane, and potatoes. Many of the early colonists had never farmed before. Their crops failed. Other colonists could not tend their farms, because they got sick from the summer heat. Some died from malaria. Malaria is an illness that causes people to have a fever and chills.

The early colonists made money by trading with the Cherokee and the Catawba. The Native Americans traded animal furs for guns and tools. The settlers sold the furs to people in England. They made coats and hats out of them.

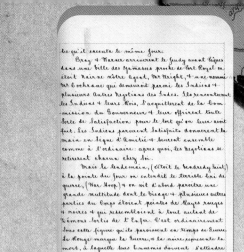

From a Letter Describing the Yamassee War

"[T]hey heard at daybreak the terrible war cry and saw at first appearing a great multitude whose faces and other parts of the body were painted in red and black rays. . . . . It is ordinarily like this that they appear in times of war. The red means war and the black represents death, which their enemies are to expect without mercy."

This letter tells of the first attack in Carolina's Yamassee War. At dawn the white settlers awoke to the shouting of the Yamassee, who were painted red and black. The letter goes on to explain that the usage and the colors of the paint mean that the Yamassee are at war.

The pirate Stede Bonnet had once been in the army. He had also owned a plantation on the island of Barbados in the Caribbean Sea. This picture of Bonnet is from a 1725 book about famous pirates. Inset: This 1715 letter describes the first attack of the Yamassee War.

Rice, Slaves, and Pirates

Around 1680, **plantation** owners in South Carolina began to grow rice. Growing rice required a lot of workers. South Carolinian rice crops depended heavily on slavery.

In 1712, Carolina was separated into North Carolina and South Carolina. Three years later the Yamassee attacked Beaufort, South Carolina. Many of its settlers died. After two years of fighting, the colonists won the war with the Yamassee.

During this time **pirates** were attacking trading ships in the area. In 1718, South Carolinian William Rhett captured the pirate Stede Bonnet. Piracy along South Carolina's coast ended after Bonnet was hanged.

In 1717, Stede Bonnet left his plantation and became a pirate. Bonnet sailed the North American coast. He captured ships and stole their contents. South Carolinian merchants whose ships Bonnet had robbed wanted him stopped. In 1718, South Carolinian William Rhett captured Bonnet. During a sea battle, Bonnet was taken to Charleston, where he was hanged.

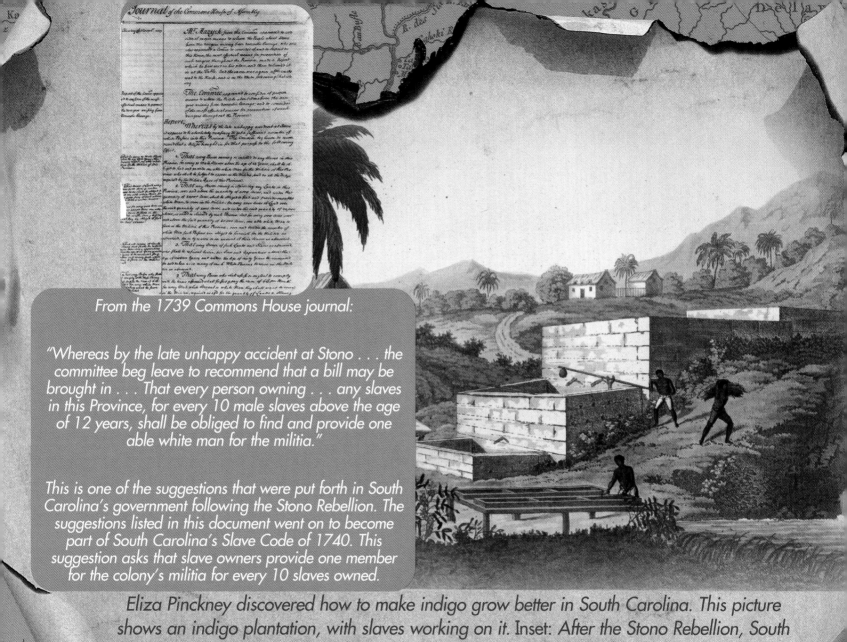

From the 1739 Commons House journal:

"Whereas by the late unhappy accident at Stono . . . the committee beg leave to recommend that a bill may be brought in . . . That every person owning . . . any slaves in this Province, for every 10 male slaves above the age of 12 years, shall be obliged to find and provide one able white man for the militia."

This is one of the suggestions that were put forth in South Carolina's government following the Stono Rebellion. The suggestions listed in this document went on to become part of South Carolina's Slave Code of 1740. This suggestion asks that slave owners provide one member for the colony's militia for every 10 slaves owned.

Eliza Pinckney discovered how to make indigo grow better in South Carolina. This picture shows an indigo plantation, with slaves working on it. Inset: After the Stono Rebellion, South Carolina's government wrote up suggestions to prevent other rebellions. These suggestions later became part of the Slave Code of 1740.

South Carolina Grows

In 1729, George I, king of Britain, made South Carolina a **royal colony**. He appointed Robert Johnson as governor. Johnson offered land to people who would settle the central part of the colony. At the time this part of the colony had few colonists.

In 1739, about 20 slaves stole guns from a store on the Stono River, near Charleston. They killed 30 white settlers before they were captured and hanged. After the Stono Rebellion, South Carolina passed slave laws.

In the 1740s, Eliza Pinckney found that **indigo** grew well in South Carolina. This gave the colony its second major crop to sell to Britain and other countries.

Eliza Pinckney was born in the West Indies in 1722. When she was 15 years old, her family moved to a plantation near Charleston. Eliza enjoyed working in the garden and seeing which types of plants grew best. One of her experiments was with indigo. It is used to make blue dye. When she found that indigo grew well in the South Carolina soil, she showed others how to plant it.

Britain borrowed money from other countries to fight the French and Indian War. When the war ended, Britain needed to pay these countries back. The war had been fought in the colonies, so Britain felt that the colonies should help pay for it. Inset: Christopher Gadsden was one of South Carolina's most outspoken objectors to Britain's rule.

Britain Taxes the Colonies

Between 1754 and 1763, Britain and France fought the **French and Indian War**. Britain beat France but then had to pay back money used to buy the guns and supplies. Britain decided to raise money by taxing the colonies.

When Britain passed the Stamp Act in 1765, the colonists became angry. This act taxed nearly all paper goods. Charleston's Christopher Gadsden spoke out against the Stamp Act. He belonged to the **Sons of Liberty**. This group hanged a dummy of a British stamp collector. The act showed their objection to the Stamp Act. It also scared the British officials in Charleston out of enforcing the Stamp Act. Gadsden **represented** South Carolina at the Stamp Act Congress held in New York City in 1765. He told the Congress that the colonists should **unite** as Americans to protest Britain's unfair taxes.

South Carolinian colonists were not happy with Britain's taxes. Many did whatever they could to avoid paying them, such as chasing away tax collectors. Inset: John Rutledge was one of South Carolina's representatives at the First Continental Congress. He was such a trusted leader that he was elected president of South Carolina from 1776 until 1778. He lived from 1739 until 1800.

South Carolina Protests Taxation

Britain did away with the Stamp Act in 1766, but continued to tax the colonies. South Carolinians protested these taxes by refusing to buy British goods. They **smuggled** them in instead. Britain tried to stop colonists from smuggling. Britain lost money when colonists did not pay taxes. Britain's taxes and attempts to stop smuggling angered some colonists. On December 16, 1773, **patriots** in Boston, Massachusetts, dumped a load of British tea into Boston's harbor. South Carolinians backed Boston's action by throwing British tea into Charleston's harbor in November 1774.

In September 1774, the colonies held the First Continental Congress in Philadelphia, Pennsylvania, to fight Britain's taxes and laws. Christopher Gadsden, John Rutledge, Edward Rutledge, Thomas Lynch, and Henry Middleton represented South Carolina.

During the Second Continental Congress, the Colonial leaders met at Independence Hall in Philadelphia, Pennsylvania. This is where the Declaration of Independence was signed. Inset: Thomas Heyward Jr. was one of South Carolina's three signers of the declaration. He lived from 1746 until 1809.

South Carolina Votes for Independence

In April 1775, the **American Revolution** began with two battles in Massachusetts. When South Carolinians heard about the battles, they raised troops to help guard the colonies.

In May 1775, leaders of the colonies met in Philadelphia for the Second Continental Congress. South Carolina was represented by the same men who had attended the first congress. During their meetings the Congress organized the Continental army. They also voted on whether the colonies should be independent of Britain. At first South Carolina's representatives voted against independence. They did not believe that the colonies were prepared to be free of British rule.

On July 4, 1776, the colonies accepted the **Declaration of Independence**. Edward Rutledge, Thomas Heyward Jr., and Arthur Middleton signed the declaration for South Carolina.

The Battle of Cowpens took place on January 17, 1781. This American win was a turning point in the Revolution. It helped speed an end to the fighting later that year. Inset: South Carolinian Francis Marion was a general in the Continental army. He was nicknamed the "Swamp Fox" because his troops would sneak attack British troops from wetlands.

The American Revolution in South Carolina

During the American Revolution, more than 100 battles were fought in South Carolina. Many of the battles were fought between the **loyalists** and the patriots living in South Carolina. Three famous South Carolinians led the patriots. They were Francis Marion, Thomas Sumter, and Andrew Pickens. In June 1776, the patriots won an important battle at Fort Moultrie. They kept the British from reaching nearby Charleston.

In 1778, the British sent troops to South Carolina. There they beat the Americans and took over the colony. In 1781, two important battles were fought in South Carolina. The Americans beat the British at Kings Mountain and at Cowpens. After these losses the weakened British troops moved to Yorktown, Virginia. In October 1781, the Americans beat the British at Yorktown, which ended the war.

The Eighth State

The American Revolution officially ended after the Treaty of Paris was signed in 1783. At the beginning of the war, the Second Continental Congress governed the colonies. Henry Middleton and Henry Laurens from South Carolina each served as president of the Congress. The colonies later followed the Articles of Confederation, which had been passed in 1777. The articles did not work for the new country after the war. They gave more power to the states than to the national government.

In 1787, the **Constitutional Convention** was held in Philadelphia to create a new government. Charles Pinckney, Charles Cotesworth Pinckney, John Rutledge, and Pierce Butler represented South Carolina. On May 23, 1788, South Carolina signed the **Constitution** and became the eighth state.

Glossary

American Revolution (uh-MER-uh-ken reh-vuh-LOO-shun) Battles that soldiers from the colonies fought against Britain for freedom, from 1775 to 1783.

Constitution (kon-stih-TOO-shun) The basic rules by which the United States is governed.

Constitutional Convention (kon-stih-TOO-shuh-nul kun-VEN-shun) A meeting of members from the 13 colonies to create a body of laws for the newly formed United States of America.

Declaration of Independence (deh-kluh-RAY-shun UV in-duh-PEN-dints) An official announcement signed on July 4, 1776, in which American colonists stated they were free of British rule.

French and Indian War (FRENCH AND IN-dee-un WOR) The battles fought between 1754 and 1763 by England, France, and Native Americans for control of North America.

indigo (IN-dih-goh) A plant that is used to make blue dye.

loyalists (LOY-uh-lists) People who were faithful to the British Crown during the American Revolution.

patriots (PAY-tree-uts) American colonists who believed in separating from British rule.

pirates (PY-ruts) People who attack and rob ships.

plantation (plan-TAY-shun) Having to do with a very large farm where crops are grown.

proprietary colony (pruh-PRY-uh-ter-ee KAH-luh-nee) A privately owned colony or settlement.

represented (reh-prih-ZENT-ed) Stood for.

royal colony (ROY-ul KAH-luh-nee) A colony whose rules were made by England.

smuggled (SMUH-gld) Sneaked something into or out of a country.

Sons of Liberty (SUNZ UV LIH-ber-tee) A group of American colonists who protested the British government's taxes and unfair treatment before the American Revolution.

unite (yoo-NYT) To bring together as a single group.

Index

Primary Sources

Page 4. Map. Colored engraving, 1630, The George A. Howard Collection. **Page 4. Inset.** *Rene Goulaine de Laudonniere and Chief Athore in front of Ribault's coulumn.* Color engraving, 16th century, Theodore de Bry, Service Historique de la Marine, Vincennes, France. **Page 6.** Map of Charles Town. 1704, South Carolina Department of Archives & History, Columbia, South Carolina. **Page 10.** *Stede Bonnet.* Woodcut, 1725, from *A General History of the Robberies and Murders of the most notorious Pyrates,* Library of Congress, Washington, D.C. **Page 10. Inset.** Letter describing the Yemassee War. May 8, 1715, George Rodd, South Carolina Department of Archives & History, Columbia, South Carolina. **Page 12. Inset.** Commons House Journal. 1739, South Carolina Department of Archives & History, Columbia, South Carolina. **Page 14. Inset.** *Chris Gadsden.* Print, circa 1800, New York Public Library, New York, New York. **Page 16. Inset.** *John Rutledge.* Oil on mahogany panel, circa 1791, attributed to John Trumbull, National Portrait Gallery, Smithsonian Institution, Washington, D.C. **Page 20.** *Colonel William Washington at the Battle of Cowpens.* Oil on canvas, 18th century, American School, Chicago Historical Society, Chicago. **Page 20. Inset.** *General Francis Marion.* Print, circa 1800, The New York Public Library, New York, New York.

Web Sites

Due to the changing nature of Internet links, PowerKids Press has developed an online list of Web sites related to the subject of this book. This site is updated regularly. Please use this link to access the list:
www.powerkidslinks.com/lotc/scarolin/